Always Shine Bright!

Alicia Bigler

Shine Bright Kids™
Choose Right. Shine Bright.

Can't-Wait Willow!

Written by
Christy Ziglar

Illustrated by
Luanne Marten

ideals children's books®
Nashville, Tennessee

ISBN-13: 978-0-8249-5648-6

Published by Ideals Children's Books
An imprint of Ideals Publications
A Guideposts Company
Nashville, Tennessee
www.idealsbooks.com

Shine Bright Kids™

Color separations by Precision Color Graphics,
Franklin, Wisconsin
Printed and bound in Canada

Library of Congress Cataloging-in-Publication Data

Ziglar, Christy.
  Can't-wait Willow! / written by Christy Ziglar ; illustrated by Luanne
Marten.
    p. cm. — (Shine bright kids)
  Summary: Willow has looked forward to seeing the Over-the-Top Circus
and enjoying treats there, but on the big day she is distracted by al sorts of
treats and fun and by the time she arrives at the circus, it is over and she
has no money left. Includes tips for parents.
  ISBN 978-0-8249-5648-6 (hardcover with jacket : alk. paper) [1.
Choice—Fiction. 2. Patience—Fiction.] I. Marten, Luanne Voltmer, ill. II.
Title. III. Title: Cannot-wait Willow!
  PZ7.Z524Can 2013
  [E]—dc23
                                    2012042176

Designed by Georgina Chidlow-Rucker
Fri_Jul13_2

To my own shining stars—
Jon, Ellie and Wes. You are
the very best! All my love.

Prov. 3:21

—CZ

DEAR GROWNUPS,

In our fast-paced, instant-gratification world, we are bombarded with dozens of choices every day. How often do we stop and take the time to think about what is most important? Without doing this, just like Willow, we may make choices that deprive our families of what is great by settling for what is merely "good enough."

As you read together, help your children recognize the "choice points"—the moments when a decision is needed. Take some time after you read the book to help them think of the choice points in their own lives. Look for ways to involve your children in day-to-day decisions, and, when appropriate, allow them to make their own choices. Talk about consequences and how one decision will impact another. Over time, they will learn how to wait for the things that are truly great!

Visit **www.AlwaysShineBright.com** for games, apps, tools, and parenting resources to help your family choose right and shine bright!

Christy Ziglar

Sometimes you need to say no. It can be better to wait. Save yes for the super amazing, and end up with the truly great!

STAR SEARCH!

Find the star that follows Willow! Can you tell whether it is excited or sad? When Willow makes wise, thoughtful decisions, the star looks happy and bright. When Willow makes choices that might not be the best, the star looks dim and deflated. On each page, notice the star's mood and try to guess why it might feel that way.

"Sometimes you've got to say 'no' to the good, so you can say 'yes' to the best."
—ZIG ZIGLAR

"Yes!" Willow shouted.
"Today's the day I've been dreaming of!
The Over-the-Top Circus is finally in town!"

Willow couldn't wait to see the elephants, the beautiful costumes, and the daring ladies on horseback.

She could already taste the delicious pink cotton candy melting on her tongue!

As she started walking toward the circus, Willow had only taken a few steps when she heard a familiar sound . . .

The ice cream truck!

The friendly driver smiled and offered her a creamy mint-chocolate-chip cone. Willow knew she needed to save her money for the circus, but . . .

Willow just
couldn't say no.

A few blocks away, Willow saw some friends playing kickball.

"Come play with us," they called.

She didn't want to miss the thrill of the ringmaster starting the circus, but . . .

Willow just couldn't say no.

After playing for a while in the hot sun, Willow was very thirsty.

A cold glass of lemonade would
certainly hit the spot. And . . .

Willow just
couldn't say no.

Willow walked and walked until she finally saw the huge circus tent.

Outside the tent, a man was offering the chance to win a purple stuffed elephant. Oooh, Willow thought, that would go perfectly in my collection. And . . .

Willow just
couldn't say no.

Willow could hear music coming from inside the tent. Next to the ticket line, there was a cage filled with colorful birds.

"Would you like to step inside?" asked the kind woman.

Willow had never seen birds like that, and . . .

Willow just couldn't say no.

Suddenly, Willow realized that it was getting very late! Inside the tent, the circus performers were doing their final act.

A lady in a polka-dot dress approached with a mountain of pink cotton candy—

at last, her favorite treat!

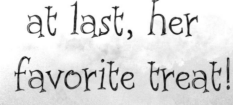

Willow reached into her pocket, only to find that she had run out of money! She had spent it all on the ice cream, the lemonade, the stuffed elephant, and the visit to the Bird House.

Now she couldn't pay for the pink cotton candy she'd been dreaming of!

Not only that, but the music had stopped and people were leaving the tent. The circus show was over!

"Oh, no!" sobbed Willow. "I've been so excited for the Over-the-Top Circus to come to town, and now

I've missed everything!"

Just then, a man in a big striped hat walked over and smiled down at Willow. "There, there," he said, trying to comfort her.

"You know, sometimes you need to learn to say no to little things that are good to end up with a big thing that is truly great!"

With that, he reached his hand into his coat pocket.

"Well, everyone deserves a second chance," he said. "I just happen to have one last ticket for tomorrow's show. Would you like to come back again tomorrow?"

Willow could hardly believe her ears . . . or her luck.

"Oh, thank you so much, sir!" she exclaimed.

The next day, Willow was ready
to go with plenty of extra time.

As she closed
the door to leave
her house, there was
that familiar sound again—
the ice cream truck!

She remembered the man
in the big striped hat . . .

And this time Willow
shook her head, **no.**

She hurried past her friends at the park.

She hurried past the lemonade stand.

She hurried past the
man in the purple booth.

She even hurried
past the Bird House.

At the circus tent, the man in the big striped hat met Willow. He was the ringmaster!

He personally escorted her to a front-row seat and announced the start of the show!

She saw the tigers and lions,
the ladies on horseback, and
the flying trapeze. She had *two*
mouthwatering pink cotton-candy treats.

And, just when she thought
her day couldn't get any better,

something
truly great
happened . . .

Willow shouted over the cheering of the crowd,

"This is SUPER AMAZING!!"